MW00947171

LOVE IS FOREVER

by Casey Rislov
illustrated by Rachael Balsaitis

CASEY RISLOV BOOKS
WYOMING • USA

To Alex, Asher, and Kylie—
May love keep you close to those you cherish most

—C. R.

For G. S. and family

—R. B.

Illustrations by Rachael Balsaitis
Design by Lois Rainwater

All inquiries or sales requests should be addressed to:

Casey Rislov Books
2405 CY Avenue
Casper, WY 82604

www.caseyrislovbooks.com
caseyrislovbooks@gmail.com

Printed and bound in the United States of America
First Edition
LCCN 2013916588
ISBN 978-0-615-88405-9

This book was expertly produced by Book Bridge Press.
www.bookbridgepress.com

A Note from the Author

Have you ever lost someone special?

Did you feel sad, angry, or confused?

Or maybe you weren't sure how to feel?

All these feelings are okay.

In this book, Little Owl loves spending time with Grandfather Owl, who teaches her many fun things. When Grandfather Owl dies, Little Owl and her family—Mama Owl, Papa Owl, and Baby Brother Owl—are very sad. But together they find a way to keep Grandfather's *love* alive.

Our *love* is a gift, a treasure to hold,
a story in our hearts forevermore.

This gift of *love* we have been given
is one that is pure, constant, and sure.

Grndpa owl
me

My affection is wider than the mountains
and deeper than the sea.
It is a *love* that will never end.

This eternal *love* binds us together as one heart,
in a life of now and in an afterlife of forever.

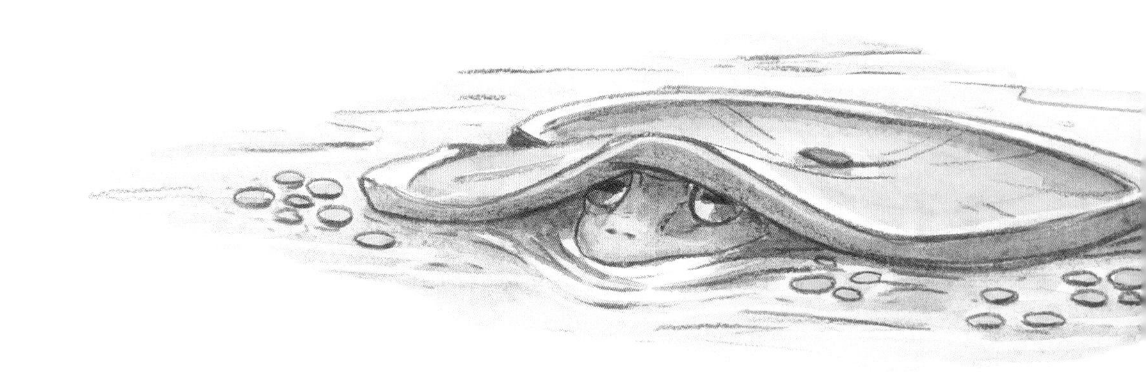

Know that my *love* will follow you always,
wherever you go and wherever you are.

Someday you may not see
me or hear me, but you can
always feel my *love*
in your heart.

GRANDPA LOVES LITTLE OWL
1
2
3
4

Love is like the brightest light that lights up
our lives and makes this life a real life.

Our tenderness for one another fills us with warmth,
a gift we are given time and again.

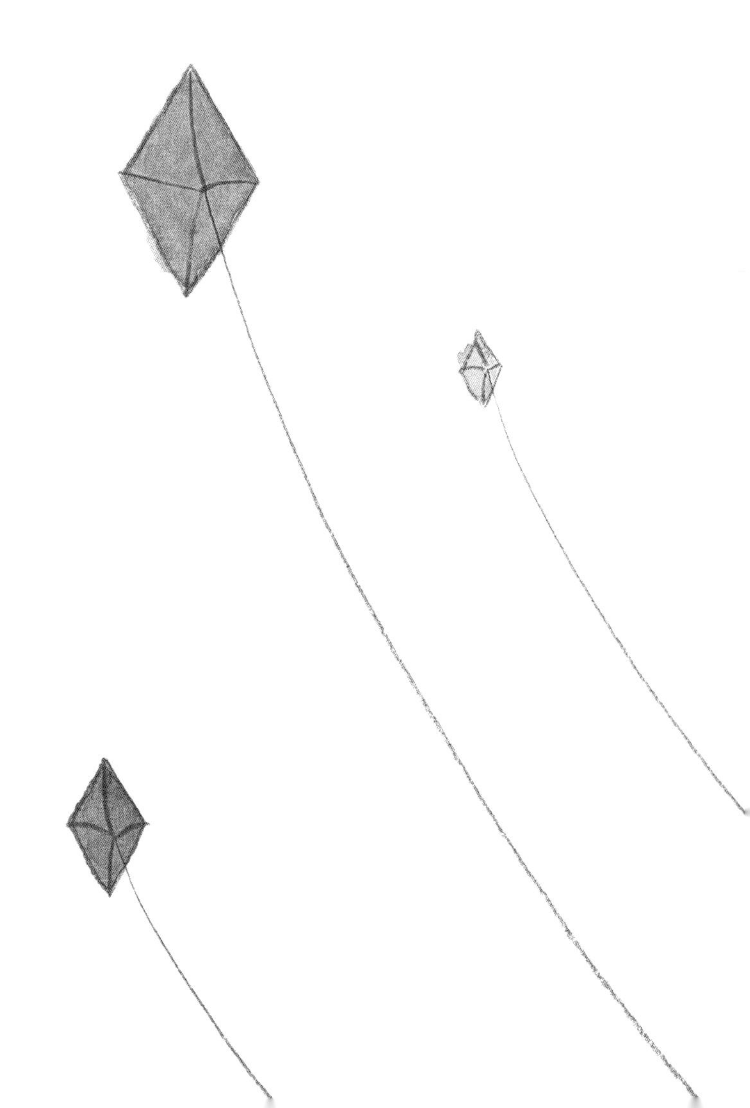

Love brings us happiness, beauty, and life.
Love is a garden that grows
with our hopes and our care.

Remember as you share, laugh, and learn,
my *love* will always be right there beside you.

TOMATO
SEED

Grandpu
owl
me
PHOTO

Family is a comfort that embraces us
and reminds us that *love* is all around.

So if a time comes when my life on Earth ends,
know that my *love*
lives from within.

My breath may cease and my body still,
but my spirit will live on with *love* all around.

My life on Earth now exists through you—
in your memories, traditions,
and always in your heart.

May your *love* for me live in all that you do.

May thoughts of me bring warmth,
just as the sun shines on you.

May your life grow as the mountains,
ever changing, ever expanding
with beauty and wonder.

May your *love* for others grow as the streams
and the rivers flow from one another.

My *love* for you will never stop.
It lives on in your laughter, in your heart, and in your thoughts.

Faith is a kind of *love* that brought me to you. Trust in this faith—
it is constant and true.

Don't think for a moment that when I'm gone
  my *love* has gone, too.

Love is a gift that binds me to you,
  a gift in your heart that is eternally true.

Grandpa Owl & me

Wherever you walk, I will walk, too.

Because my *love* will live forever in you.

From the Experts

ROBERT VIGNERI, MD

As a pediatrician, parents ask me for advice about children dealing with the loss of a loved one. I encourage parents to talk to their children about their loss and reassure them that it is okay to feel sad and to cry. It is important to remember that the person lives on not only in our memories, but in the lessons they have taught us and the family traditions they have passed to the next generation.

REV. CYNTHIA DOBSON MCBRIDE

Talking to children about death

- Use simple, honest, direct language. Use the word "died," not "sleeping."
- Answer all questions honestly and in simple terms (even the difficult ones). Provide only as much detail as the child requests.
- Allow children to express their feelings and ask questions. They may express raw, strong emotions (yelling, crying, wailing) or be very quiet. Help them process the death over an extended period of time.
- Tell your child what will happen in the next few days. (If the body is suitable for viewing, and the death is someone close to the child, allow children to see the body if they want to. Let them know ahead of time what to expect.)
- Give your child choices whenever possible. Some children find it comforting to continue normal routines (such as going to school). If you are a parent, be aware that what is right for one child may be different for his or her sibling.
- Reassure your children that they are safe.

Should children attend funerals?

Depending on the age of your child, it is appropriate to discuss the service ahead of time and let your child decide what he or she wants to do. At any age, grief and how it is expressed is unique for each individual. While some children may prefer not to attend a funeral or memorial service, others will want to attend and find it meaningful. Preschoolers often find it difficult to sit still during a long service. If the deceased is the child's parent or other very close loved one, even if the child is too young to remember much later, it may be meaningful when children are older to know that they were included in some way and had a chance to say goodbye. If you have an active toddler you choose to take to a service, it can be helpful to have a friend or relative on hand to assist with his or her care if needed.

Talk with your children before going to the funeral home or cemetery so they will know what to expect. Will there be a time of viewing or visitation before the service? Will there be an open casket, and will the children see a body? If so, explain in your own words that the person is not in any pain, they're not hurting, or hungry, or cold. If the funeral is part of a religious service, invite the officiant or a trusted adviser to speak directly with your child. If cremation was chosen, explain that there was no pain during the cremation. If your child wants to, allow him or her to see the ashes.

If the service is for a close relative of the child, invite her or him to participate in some simple way. This may mean writing (and or reading) a brief letter, poem, or story about the loved one. They could sing a lullaby or favorite song, or say a short prayer—either at the visitation or during the service. Some children will be most comfortable with no visible role at all, but it is important for them to find their own way to say goodbye. Trust your children to know what is best for their own needs.

A good general guideline is to know that most children appreciate being given the opportunity to decide for themselves about participating in services. Remember that grief is an ongoing journey. On special occasions in the future, such as on the anniversary date of a loved one's passing, on birthdays, or at holidays, you may choose to find a special way to help your child remember his or her loved one and process his or her grief. You could set a place at a family meal, visit a grave and place flowers or a wreath, write

a brief note or letter, sing a song, or light a candle. Allow your children to talk about those who have died whenever they want or need to. Take care of your own emotional health and seek support from others.

KELSEY DONNINI, LCSW

Children will experience a wide variety of feelings when a loved one dies. Children may feel sad, angry, scared, lonely, confused, anxious, or somewhat disconnected. Death and loss are difficult for adults to process, and can be even more difficult for children. Children will learn how to grieve and cope with death from watching and experiencing it alongside those who care for them.

Open and honest communication is the key to beginning the process of grieving and healing. Allow children to express their feelings in child-friendly ways such as art, singing, talking, asking questions, or reading books about dying and loss. Help children understand and trust that their feelings are normal and helpful by naming and acknowledging those feelings. Use empathy to help children realize they are not alone in their feelings. Try to understand, and not fix, how they are feeling. Let them know that you also have these feelings, and the feelings come and go, and change over time.

Be honest with children about the permanency of death and avoid telling children their loved one is "away" or "sleeping." Children will have many questions about where their loved one is and will want to ask questions about the afterlife. These discussions will bring hope to a hurting child and in many cases will help them find closure.

One of the best ways to cope with a death or loss is sharing memories and creating family rituals about the loved one who died. Create a memory book, or look through old photos. Laugh about the silly things the person did. Do something in remembrance of the loved one by planting a tree or flowers, volunteer, or give a donation to the person's favorite charity.

All people experience and process death and loss at different speeds, with different coping skills, and with different understanding. Do not be surprised if you begin to see an increase in emotional behavior, tantrums, or unexplainable behavior months after the loss occurred. It can take a significant amount of time for children to process and begin to understand the life-changing effect death can have on a family. Understand that this behavior is not misbehavior, but a call for help that says, "I am ready and need help understanding my feelings."

Conversations about death and loss can be difficult, particularly when the adults in the family are also grieving. Some of the questions below might be helpful in starting those difficult conversations that will begin the journey to healing and peace.

- Who is a person you know who has died?
- What do you know about what happens to people when they die?
- How do you feel about the person dying? Sad, angry, confused, scared? Unsure?
- Do you wonder about where the person is now?
- What are your favorite memories of the person?
- How would you like to remember the person?
- How can I best help you right now?

Resources

Books and Journals

Angel Catcher: A Journal of Loss and Remembrance
by Kathy Eldon and Amy Eldon Turteltaub

Angel Catcher for Kids: A Journal to Help You Remember the Person You Love Who Died
by Amy Eldon

Help Me Say Goodbye: Activities for Helping Kids Cope When a Special Person Dies
by Janis Silverman

The Invisible String
by Patrice Karst, illustrated by Geoff Stevenson

Lifetimes: The Beautiful Way to Explain Death to Children
by Bryan Mellonie and Robert Ingpen

On Grief and Grieving: Finding the Meaning of Grief Through the Five Stages of Loss
by Elisabeth Kubler-Ross and David A. Kessler

Water Bugs and Dragonflies: Explaining Death to Young Children
by Doris Stickney, illustrated by Gloria Claudia Ortiz

You can find additional books and websites at
The New York Life Foundation • AChildinGrief.com

Websites

Children's Grief Education Association • childgrief.org

The Dougy Center • dougy.org

Helpguide.org • helpguide.org/mental/grief_loss.htm

Kidsaid • kidsaid.com

Mayo Clinic • mayoclinic.com/health/grief/MH00036

The New York Life Foundation • AChildinGrief.com

PBS.org • pbs.org/thisemotionallife/topic/grief-and-loss

PubMed Health • ncbi.nlm.nih.gov/pubmedhealth/PMH0002497

More Help

Clergy, mental health specialists, self-help groups, social workers,
pediatrician, school counselor, local hospital

CASEY RISLOV holds a master's degree in elementary education and is endorsed in early childhood and special needs. She taught for many years at a local developmental preschool and currently stays home with her two young children. Casey's first book, *Time Together, Time Well Spent!* (November 2011), allowed her to share her love of reading and teaching with many local students. And she is excited to now share a tender side of herself through her new book, *Love Is Forever.*

Casey lives with her family in Wyoming, where she enjoys spending time in the mountains, downhill skiing, boating, and water skiing—and reading and writing, of course!

RACHAEL BALSAITIS studied illustration at the Minneapolis College of Art and Design, where she discovered her love of illustrating for children. Born in Duluth, Rachael grew up in rural Minnesota and has been drawing since the day she could hold a crayon. *Love Is Forever* by Casey Rislov is her first picture book.

Rachael lives with her four rats in the Twin Cities, where she can be found bicycling, illustrating, and waiting out the snowy winters with a stack of books.